ANGEL
and ADAM

ANGEL and ADAM
Copyright © 2022 by DAVID G. BICKLER

Published in the United States of America
ISBN   Paperback: 978-1-959761-36-5
ISBN   eBook: 978-1-959761-37-2

All rights reserved. No part of this publication may be reproduced, stored in a retrieval system or transmitted in any way by any means, electronic, mechanical, photocopy, recording or otherwise without the prior permission of the author except as provided by USA copyright law.

The opinions expressed by the author are not necessarily those of ReadersMagnet, LLC.

ReadersMagnet, LLC
10620 Treena Street, Suite 230 | San Diego, California, 92131 USA
1.619. 354. 2643 | www.readersmagnet.com

Book design copyright © 2022 by ReadersMagnet, LLC. All rights reserved.

Cover design by Ericka Obando
Interior design by Daniel Lopez

ANGEL and ADAM

DAVID G. BICKLER

ReadersMagnet, LLC

Dedication

My brother Robert and I dedicate this story to our children Kristin, Kelsey I, Jared, Zane, Justine, Kelsey II, Caleb, and Cameron.

May you always remember words inspired by the love of God.

This story was written with the inspired spirit shared by our parents and their teachings, with the energy flowing within, as Robert and I have dedicated our love to our own children and families, as well as to the families and the beautiful children of our readers. We want to follow God's example of unconditional love. We feel in our heart of hearts that this story of love is our spirits, sharing a story about love, and especially God's love. We both dedicate this to all the children of the earth, and all the children known to God. The children of the men and women of God are our future may God bless them, and us all.

With honor, love, and peace we dedicate this to our ancestors, our mothers and fathers from the beginning of time. We dedicate it also to all mothers and fathers currently living, and to all of our friends both within and outside our family, we thank you. We love you all.

Love is all we really have.

ANGEL AND ADAM

DAVID G. BICKLER

*ALSO WRITTEN BY OUR FAMILY,
IN HONOR OF LOVE*

God's Love Machine by *Joseph Buechler*

Time to Choose by *David G. Bickler*

Sex, Lies & Dreams by David G. Bickler

ANGEL AND ADAM

HELLO YOU, THERE! With a clash crash roar of thunder, with bright flashes of lightning, and many blazing colors, this is the voice of God. I am the first God ever to be, and you will all see in these words written about the very beginning of everything, long before time, I was just thinking about you. I was thinking about *all* of you who would soon be. There I was, sitting all alone I was so far, far away, and so alone. I was very alone. Long before this particular pinpoint of time where we all simply began, I was so all alone. You see, I am in your dreams I need you, I want to be closer to you, more than just a dream, for I am you. This you will see, so here we go…here I come, and this you will see.

A long time ago, God was sitting around, doing whatever God does in his/her sitting, and thinking: "Self, you have been alone for such a long time, sitting out here in the darkness so far, far away, and so very alone. I see you have nobody to play with; you have no one to talk to or love, or to create with. I am so alone with myself. I am all the love there is, but so all alone. I am everything there is or can ever be, but I am still so all alone. As I sit in my thoughts about this creation, all by myself, I think how wonderful it would be so grand, so wonderful, so full of love, so very beautiful if only I had a friend to share all I Am, a friend to play with…someone just like me. Just think of the things I could do with another soul made from myself an identical twin God just like me, just like you will be.

"This twin would be a pure individual I could teach my new self everything I know. This is what I want to share. I will share all the things I've made with my new self, for I did create this beautiful place, this universe we see, with all my imagination of love, peace, and beauty for you to see. Everything you see was created with my love, and it is so beautiful. I will share all of it with another soul, another me, who can give so much of the same love and joy I'm made of. It will be so beautiful, so nice to share my creation. I will share myself with you: we are one and the same, and this is what we share. You are me and I am you….

"Then we could sit forever in our time as we talk about all of my second self's new experiences. These would be all the experiences I enjoyed while thinking of you all oh, look at what you can do, for you can do what I can do! I made you from myself, as you will all see. I will sit by in the heavens above; I will sit in silence as I watch my new child, and you, my new friends, my children from myself. My child will light up like me, and so will you, with all the brilliance of white, yellow, silver, blue, and gold…all the colors in our universe, like the rainbows that we see in reflections of the sun. You will all see this, for this is me. This is my new self and all of you will see as my new self explores the beauty of all these things, as my new self sees the universe for the very first time. My new me is glowing with love, her wings of pale gold feathers flapping in the sun. My new self and I will never fade away, for I am she now, and she is me. I will never fade away from you or from my new self. I will watch my new young friend fly around this will make me smile. Oh, how you've made me glow, from showing your love while you grow and glow. I sit and watch you shine each moment of each day, in the glory of you and all I've made.

"My new self has such a puzzled smile on her face, a look of frustration as she tries to learn all the things that there are to learn and to be enjoyed, for what she sees and what you all will see is all my love, which I display. I will also see your life through you and your eyes. We made the world you see as one, together in this place I have made. The greatest joy I have in me is to see her, my new self, solving the answers in all those wonderful things I've made for her and you, in all these things she will encounter, as you will see throughout my universe and yours was made just for you all, and you will see me."

As God's new self was out and exploring all these new and magi cal wonderful things, God thought about all of this for a while. God could see and feel that God's new self would need a friend. "This new friend will be my soul mate…just maybe one of you. Hmmm! I wonder… how should this new soul or person be from me? What will it be, this new you of me was created to be my first child." This was no puzzler for a God of love and peace. For God to create anything was quite easy, for God had already created it all. If God wanted a cookie, or a game, a boat or basketball or train, a kite or a puppy or two, or a goldfish or a kitten, then anything God might want or need would simply appear like a magic trick at a show. From God's pure, loving thought, anything he wanted simply appeared. If God thought about a blanket, or anything at all, with no effort it would just appear. These were all easy things for God to do, for God could do anything. But these items were just objects just playthings, simple things. They couldn't talk, or love, or create; they couldn't play ball or giggle, jump rope or laugh. These toys were just things that couldn't feel or show love. They all looked nice and pretty, and were fun to play with, but they just sat around him with their beauty on display. So God sat and prayed about the creation of a soul mate, which would require much more thought than just a few cookies and toys. For Love was his final toy to make.

A long time had passed. Now God was getting ready to make a new friend. God was getting really excited, for this was to be a great new friend. "Myself I made of me now will finally have the perfect friend to play with, to explore everything that I created from my love, and from my teachings," God said. And on this day of God's excitement, God started to visualize in her mind the perfect soul to be. "Just as my first self was my first child, so my second will be like you and me, and this you will see."

With her eyes closed, God thought about everything her soul mate would have the same simple things, like love, joy, happiness, compassion, a few smiles, the ability to imagine all possibilities, with a little dash of choice, plus just a touch of forgetfulness.

"With love so grand, what a perfect soul mate to be as perfect as you all will be," said God. When God opened her eyes, there stood before her the most beautiful perfect soul you might say she looked like an angel. "Oh, how is she so perfect?" God cried with joy. His heart swelled with even more love from what she had made. This was better than she could ever have imagined, for making another was so very, very special, as you will see.

As God cried over this new soul, something happened that was very new and different. God felt a warm, tingly feeling deep down inside, and then she started to glow with a bright light. It was so wonderful there was so much joy, that God just had to experience this again.

The new soul asked, as the first one had, "But what is this wonderful feeling that we are both feeling?"

God thought, *I know what warmth is, and I know what happiness is, and I know what peace is, but this is so tingly all over, inside and out!* Somehow, God had never felt this feeling before; in all his creations, this was the best he ever felt. It was so wonderful that he knew he must always remember and share it.

"But what shall we call it?" asked the new soul.

"I know," said God. "I shall call this feeling LOVE, and when I feel it again, I will always know it is LOVE. When you feel this pure Love inside, this will always be my Love."

The new soul stood before God a new soul mate who did not yet have a name. In all of God's excitement, she completely forgot about a name for the new soul mate. God thought about all of this for a while, and finally came up with a wonderful idea for her new friend's name. "I shall call her Angel yes, that is the name. She is the Angel of Love." Oh, how God enjoyed this new name, and this new feeling of Love, which God wanted to be reminded of each and every day. God would never let the Angel of Love go.

As God was standing there thinking, this new soul, Angel, was sitting by and also thinking, looking around, not really sure what was going on in her new place. A picture popped into her mind of some thing that must be her father or mother, so she said to God, "Are you my mommy?"

God laughed and said, "Yes, my Angel, I am your father as well as your best friend, your soul mate, your playmate, and your mom my, too. I am Love and life, for I have made you from me." It was funny… God hadn't used words before, as they had always talked to each other just in thought mostly, it seemed. It was strange to talk with a voice.

"What were you thinking about?" asked the new soul.

"I was thinking about what I should call you a name that would mean everything. In all I've made with all my Love, this name would be perfect, like you, so that when I called your name you would know to come to me when I pray," replied God.

"Oh, so what shall my name be?" she asked, with a big, perfect smile, ear to ear, full of excitement that God could see.

"Your name is Angel. You are the Angel of Love. All my love I show is you, my dear you are my Angel. This is you," replied God.

"I like my name," answered Angel. "This name is perfect, as God is perfect. Now, what shall we do?"

With a quick flash and bang, God swept her away, and then he said, "Let's go exploring. I want to show you all the things I've made."

And off they went, God and Angel, hand in hand, heart in heart, swirling lights flashing here and there. They swiftly went off to see everything God had created for his new self, and for all of you, too.

II.

GOD WAS VERY happy as she watched Angel fly around and play, as Angel explored the universes made for you and for her. As you will learn, she was learning all there is to learn, with all I've made for all to see. Together they explored the heavens, as far as the heavens extended, with all the creatures roaming on the planets of all the gal axies in all the solar systems of God's creation. As you will do, this Angel filled the air with Love, and with happiness and so much joy in caring. She was certainly giving and sharing all these things of God that she had found. Oh, how she did play, as she learned how won derful God's imagination is, how his Love is, and what his devotion to creation really means pure as the sun and rain, the oceans and seas, and all the trees. The discoveries Angel made in God's universe were endless each discovery would fill the air with Angel's thoughts, her feelings, and her Love. God's Love made her shine with her angel's wings of gold and silver as she dropped Love everywhere she went. Angel was creating, just as God had done.

Now, did you know that Angel was created from God's imagination, and from God's heart of pure Love? Angel was now part soul, part spirit, but mostly pure Love. Angel is the universe of God's Love, and that Love is in all of you, too. You are made from Love, the very same beautiful thing that made God and Angel. However, in God's devotion, he/she could see that Angel did not have a human body, yet she had a smile within her glowing light. She didn't have a complete body like some of God's creations that she saw playing in the uni verses that God had made, but don't you worry Angel's body would come later. Angel could not feel anything inside yet as we do on Earth, because Angel was still pure, brilliant light of all those beautiful colors. She was made up of colors, with a smile, just like God. Her feelings were shown on the outside, where she and God could clearly see them. If you could see Angel and God together, they would look like the colors of the rainbow. You look like that to God, too the col ors you display tell God a story about you, each and every day, so he can be with you in sorrow or happiness each and every day.

God was filled with so much love and joy, and his happiness for Angel was so bright. Just then, God experienced something she really was not expecting. Every time Angel made a new discovery, as Angel lit up with her smile, God would see the colors of her smile. He could feel the joy inside he felt her love. Angel knew why God loves us all. Every time Angel would do a kind thing for one of God's creatures, Angel's love would shine brightly around her, and then God would light up even brighter than usual. God could see this he could feel it inside his heart just as Angel could. This reminded God of that first day when God made Angel, when Angel came into God's life. The same Love made her feel very warm, tingly, and complete. This made God cry with such happiness, for he felt that Angel's Love was pure, true Love. Angel felt God's Love, and God felt Angel's Love in return. They both watched as the heavens started to shine. The heavens were full of rainbows that day, all around God himself, and Love was all around Angel. Her Love, and God's Love, were now pure for all to share this you will see.

As time went on, Angel continued to explore the heavens. Angel would watch God smile as she smiled, and she would laugh as God laughed. They loved laughing together. Sometimes Angel would do really kind acts for God's creatures. These beautiful things that Angel would do, God would notice, for he notices everything we do. Oh, how God would start to glow with the magnificence of a bright star as Angel loved all the things in our universe as God does. They both glowed in the harmony of life and Love.

Then one day, Angel saw God start to glow again just a little brighter, adding to her already glowing magnificence. Angel was really curious about this and asked God, "Why do you glow so beautifully? Sometimes it seems as though you glow brighter with each day."

God replied, "Dear loved one, my sweet Angel, it makes me happy to see you happy. It makes me smile when you smile."

"But I do not understand why you glow so wonderfully?" asked Angel.

"This glow you see is the Love I see that surrounds you as you explore, as you play. I glow, as you see, because it makes me happy how you learn, how you smile, with the Love I taught, which I see all around you. It makes me happy that you show compassion for all living things. You Love as I Love."

Then Angel asked, "Does it hurt? Because sometimes, I see you weeping."

"Oh, no! My little Angel, my dear loved one, what you see is the Love I feel inside of me coming from your Love, which makes me glow."

Angel was puzzled by this idea of Love; it was a lot harder to understand than other things in the universe. She couldn't figure out how God could feel this Love inside when she herself could not feel this Love like her father did. *I know his Love, but I know there's even more*, she thought. She knew it was real; she could see it all around God, all around herself, but she couldn't understand what love felt like. All she really knew was that she must be Love, because her name was Angel of Love, and God had made her.

Angel started thinking this over. She wondered how she might feel this Love it looked so beautiful, so warm. God was so happy with this Love. *Surely I too must be able to feel the same…I see God enjoying Love. I should be able to feel this Love too. After all, I did come from God, who is my mommy, who created me. This would make me just like her I know I should feel it too.* Thinking about this, Angel realized that she didn't really feel things at all. She had learned everything there was to know about the universe, and she understood that she was part of the whole universe, but she was puzzled about these feelings of love.

After several moments of thinking this through, the little soul named Angel asked God another question. "God, I've thought this through. I know I can see Love, because I see it all around you, and I know that I am Love, because you said that it comes from me know ing you. God, what I would really like is to feel Love, just like you. I would like to feel the warmth you feel, as well as even the tears you cry. God, I'm sure that if I can feel as you do, and if I know all these things about Love, then I will know Love, and who I am. I know I will be just like you because of the way you feel Love and the way you have given me Love."

So Angel prayed to God. "Will I always be your rainbow's colors?"

In an instant, God spoke to Angel. "No, my child I have much more to show you in your life's display."

God was so overcome with joy and Love so grand from this little soul's request that suddenly God turned into a bright light of bril liance she ignited into the most magnificent ray of light. This light was so bright that Angel had a hard time seeing God, but he was there his presence was in the light, which Angel also became part of. The little soul closed her eyes; she lay down for just a moment or two, and then she prayed to God. She told God that she was scared.

"The light is so bright I can no longer see. Where are you, God?" Angel felt heavy and somewhat tired. Angel was starting to feel very uncomfortable she hadn't felt this before…so heavy, like a big rock.

God spoke to the little soul to comfort her. He began to explain to Angel that she had been given a very special gift. God reminded her that she had started out as a spirit from Love, pure energy, and that they had played together in this sweet light until Angel had learned all there was to know, for until then, she could not be born.

"You see, my sweet Angel, we must be the light of Love. You must be all my light of Love before you become the flesh of my creation, and before you can receive this body of flesh. You see, then I can make you whole. Dear loved one, you asked to feel what Love is like in human form you wondered what Love is like then, you wanted to feel its warmth in your heart. I will be with you in your heart every day. Dear loved one, I have given you the tools to do everything that you ask, so that you will feel you know all my Love. When you find my Love, you will know who you are, and you will always remember who I am. For I am you we were always one and the same.

"Now listen I will watch you from heaven above while you play. Angel, now try to go to sleep, my child, and I will finish making you in my physical image. After you rest, you will awaken. You will then see with your eyes these eyes will be how you see shapes. They will see all we have made while you were in the light with me as we first soared through the heavens. You will feel heavy not light like the butterflies, but heavy like a rock. You will move slowly, but you can run, skip, and even jump or climb, but you will be able to hear. You will also hear with your silly little ears you will hear sounds you haven't ever heard. Your button nose will smell the aromas of the universe, and not only that your mouth will be made of wonderful ways for you to taste so many flavorful things. You know we can't do any of those things unless we come here to play.

"You will experience emotions, many sensations that are powerful inside, for these feelings in a body can be quite loud. These feelings, sights, and sounds, are to help guide you in your life choices as you teach and play. In this life you have now, you will have free will, free choice. Guided by choices of Love, your heart will guide you, because you know Love will let you grow. You will have thought, imagination, and memory. This will be confusing to you as you grow, but do not fear, because if you feel fear or if you feel lost, then you will forget who you are. I am always here; your life is guided by my Love that I've placed secretly for you in each and every day. Remember in your worry or your play, just look up to me and know I am always here for you. I have given you all of these things, which may confuse you in many ways, just as you have asked, just as you were before your flesh body, which we made for you to play.

"I will always be on the path of Love in your every day. As well, there will be miracles for you. Every day, you will always feel in your heart of Love that I am there for you. I have also given you a brother a partner, so to speak, to keep you company while you play. You will show your brother all there is to explore with you along your way. You will find comfort in your brother's arms, just as you did in mine, for he was made of pure Love, just like you and me. Together you will feel in your hearts that I am always here watching you live, watching you grow. I am in you we are one.

"Now show me what you feel show me how you both can love each other as you play. I am sorry to fly away, but I must go for now, for I have to close the doors to heaven. You have much yet to do here on Earth. This is your new home for now, but do not fear heaven is your home, too. Earth is where I have placed you with your brother, but your home our home in heaven will always be there for you to return to, as well as all of you. So Angel, take your partner go now, go and play with all we have made.

"Once again, as you go into the world, try to remember that the window to heaven will always be open just a little, for you to see me as well. This is true for everyone, as you will see. You can peek in anytime with a prayer. I will hear you pray, and I will answer when you pray. I will come to you in many of my many ways. So if you feel lonely, take a peek inside. You will see that I am there, waiting for you, loving you, and watching you play, watching you share, watch ing you talk of me, sharing our Love for all to see what they can be.

"I must tell you now that I've placed a veil over the window. Let's just say it's a blanket or curtain, just behind the window a little, just to keep my bright light of Love and joy from blinding you while you peek in the window. If you were to see all of my Love that I have for you, the flash of light would blind you. You would forget about why you were made and why I put you out there to play, for when you do come home to Heaven, our brilliant lights of Love will blend together and we will become one in heaven. Then we will review everything you did when you played."

And with that, God said goodbye. He/she closed the door to the little soul's memory of her home.

"Angel, this will always be your home," he said. "Go play I will never go away.

III.

ANGEL WAS AWAKENED from her deep sleep. She felt that a very bright light was shining in front of her. She could feel the warmth com ing from this brightness, this yellow ball of warmth this huge bright ball was floating in the distance far, far away in the skies above… wow. This ball was so warm; it felt like God's Love. This bright red orange ball reminded her of a time when she used to play in the light, but couldn't recall its warmth being so close. It was as though the warmth were inside her, this time. Then Angel opened her eyes. For the first time, she was blinded by the light. She quickly closed her eyes. Seeing this light, she was reminded again of a time when she could look at it in joy, but this light was so much brighter it kind of hurt to look at it for too long. Angel tried again to open her eyes, but first she moved slightly away from it so it wouldn't blind her.

She glanced at it, squinting. *Odd*, she thought. *I don't recall mov ing so slowly.* Again she opened her eyes this time, it was much better. As Angel lay there in the cool grass, with the ocean crashing in the distance, she thought about all these new sensations, these overwhelming feelings. She slowly became sleepy. Overwhelmed by her new sense of sight, she drifted back to sleep.

In her dreams, she remembered a time of being in the light, feeling and knowing great joy and warmth oh, how freely and fast she could move in that time! But this new body and new place were so different from what she remembered when she played and danced with God in the light. This was an indescribable sensation. It seemed to come from somewhere inside her new body. It was a wonderful feeling. It felt so… tingly. It was very pleasant.

As Angel continued to lie there in the grass, dreaming of everything that had taken place, a strange sadness moved through her. This sadness made her feel as if she were missed, or as if she were missing someone. This feeling of sadness brought on another feeling of loneliness. It was a moving dream oh, how she longed to be held. During her dream, she heard a voice say, "Angel, do not be sad. I love you. As promised, I have given you a brother to keep you company. He is there to hold you. He will comfort you. His name is Adam. Now, remember to love him as you love me show him all you know. I love you, Angel."

Angel stirred in her sleep at the sound of her name. When she opened her eyes, she saw someone standing there calling out to her, "Angel, Angel wake up! Let's go play!" Adam reached out and took Angel's hand. Angel noticed how nice and soft it felt and it glowed a bit. Then Adam pulled Angel to her feet and into his arms. He said, "Angel, I have missed you so much." He hugged her for a long while. Then he smiled at her and asked if she would like to go for a swim.

"Maybe after we swim, we can explore the countryside," he said. So Adam and Angel set off for their swim in the warm lake.

Crystal Lake was a lake of pure holy water. It was located in a nice green valley, and fed by a gentle waterfall from the mountains. The lake was bordered by a forest to the east where the sun rises, and beautiful mountains stretching to the west where the sun sets over the ocean blue. The forest and mountains met each other in the south and all the way to the north, forming a circle around the lake. The sky was always blue, and the lake was never chilly just warm. The open land was covered in a carpet of short and tall grasses so many shades of green, all mixed together. This was a special place of beauty like no other on earth; it was a pure place.

Adam and Angel would spend many years in this place, for it was like heaven, as Angel felt as they sat watching the sunrises and sunsets, which were so beautiful each and every day. This was Angel's

favorite thing to do. Every time she saw a sunset, she would hear music within herself. The music told her that God was with her. Every time she saw the sunrise, she felt warmth, and the Love of God was the music played in the sunrise and sunset every day.

In the forest, they would watch birds fly as they listened to them sing and play. Within the forests there were furry animals running all around on the forest floor for them to chase and play with. Angel's favorite animal was the rabbit. She loved to feed them, as she watched their little noses wiggle, as they ate and sniffed the air. When Angel held them, she noticed that they felt was soft as the clouds in the heavens she was amazed by how soft they were. Adam was proud of the deer, the elk, and the moose. Adam was most fond of the creatures that played in the forest, where they all played. They were a challenge for Adam in his play, and he would try to outrun or outjump them every day.

Some days, Angel and Adam would explore the mountains. It was always a magical time. There were always new and beautiful places to see, and exciting places to explore so many trails, caves, and rivers, and trees that seemed as big as mountains. One of their favorite games in the mountains was called "mountain goat jump." They both would jump from rock to rock like the goats they saw. The rules of the game were that they must jump from rock to rock without falling off or touching the ground. If they did fall off, they would have to start over at the edge of the boulder field. The first one to the other side got to pick the ripe strawberries that grew there.

Angel was very good at jumping from rock to rock, but she would always let her brother win, because Angel knew that when Adam won, he would pick the strawberries first. Now, this was the fun part for Angel, because you know what? He would always wait for Angel to get there, to let her choose the strawberries she wanted to eat. He didn't know why he did this he just knew that he had a warm feeling inside when he let her have first choice from the berries he picked.

He didn't mind, because she always chose the same big juicy berries that he would have chosen for her. It made him smile when he saw how much she liked them even better was the fact that she saved the last, the very largest and juiciest, for him.

IV.

ANGEL AND ADAM spent many, many years in the valley called Heaven on Earth. They were so happy sharing, playing, and growing together. As Angel and Adam grew older, they started doing things on their own. Adam continued to explore the mountains; he really liked the challenge of climbing, exploring caves, running and skipping, exploring the deep valleys and the mountain peaks. There were so many beautiful things he enjoyed all the shapes, the colors within the rocks many things glowed with God's Love. Angel seemed to prefer the forest, where she was very relaxed. She learned how to take care of the animals when they were wounded, and she would help lost babies to find their mothers. This gave her great joy inside. Somehow, it all seemed familiar, as if she'd done this before.

One evening, after watching the sunset paint its colors all over the sky, as the visions she saw in the heavens played their music in Angel's heart, Angel turned to Adam and asked, "Why do you sit so quietly tonight with that worried look on your face?"

Adam turned to Angel, wanting to explain how he was feeling. "Angel, I found a cave on the side of a mountain, deep in one of the valleys where I love to play. I was curious about what might be inside, but it was dark…oh, so very dark. I couldn't see very far into the cave at all. I wanted to get a better look, so I started walking into the open ing. When I stepped past the entrance to the cave, there was a voice calling out. I stopped to listen, but couldn't hear anything coming from the cave. I took a few more steps into the cave, and then I heard the voice again."

"What did the voice say to you, Adam?"

"I'm not really sure, Angel. I was confused my heart was racing, pumping very fast as though I were running. I kept looking around, but couldn't see a figure or anyone talking. I knew it wasn't you you were in the forest with the animals. All I can remember is that it said something like 'Be careful,' and 'Remember when the darkness is of temptation.'"

Adam was surely shaken by this, but Angel did not know whether it was from hearing the voice, or from what he could not see in the cave. Angel remembered hearing voices in her dreams, for that was how she had known she would have a brother, but this did not shake her up as it had Adam. So she asked Adam why he felt upset.

"Adam, were you shaken up by the voice that you could not see, or by the darkness of the cave?"

"I don't know, Angel. The voice was calm…somewhat peaceful. The darkness of the cave lessened with each step, as I waited for my eyes to adjust to the darkness, but still nothing was visible. I think I'm worried because of what the voice said: 'Be careful, Adam. Try to re member what's in your heart.' I felt as though something was going to happen. We need to be careful and try to remember something. I felt happiness, but sadness at the same time." Then Adam said, "Angel, would you come with me to the cave tomorrow? I feel like we both should go there. I would really like to see what's inside."

Angel said, "Sure, Adam I will go with you to the cave, and on the way we can play mountain goat. We haven't done that in a long time."

"Thanks, Angel. I feel a little better, but I still have this feeling that we need to watch out for something." Then Adam lay down and closed his eyes. He was very tired and sleepy from the long day hik ing and playing in the mountains. Angel was starting to get sleepy too, so she walked over to her place in the grass where she would lie down and rest.

Sara, Angel's new friend, curled up alongside her. Angel found her one day while out in the forest. Sara looked so tired, and very hungry, but happy to see Angel. She was a small four legged creature, similar to what we know today as a dog what a sweet little puppy. Sara was white as snow, with a spot or two; she was as soft as a rabbit or hamster. Sara's eyes were as beautiful as Angel's they shone just like Adam's eyes. As you know, Angel was very good at helping the animals of the forest and of the earth, so she took poor Sara home. She cared for her with all her Love, like God's Love, just as God loves us all. Sara hadn't left Angel's side since that day she was her friend, very loyal hearted. Soon Angel fell into a deep sleep. As she lay there in her cozy warm bed, she began to have a dream.

In this dream, she saw herself standing before a warm, white light. This light was talking to her she had heard this voice before. She didn't see a face or mouth, but she could hear everything the light

was saying. This didn't frighten Angel, because it was very comforting to be in the light. As she was standing there in her dream, the light said to her, "Dear loved one, my sweet Angel oh, how I love you so much. It makes me so happy to see you enjoying earth, with all the things we have made. It fills me with great joy, the way you take care of my creatures of the forest, and of our planet. I am filled with your love when you let your brother Adam win at the games you play on the rocks. Angel, you are about to learn something. It is something you have always wanted to feel something your heart is yearning for. My Angel, when you feel this emotion, it will tingle…this feeling will vibrate throughout your whole body, and your spirit will light up. When this happens, Angel, you will remember who you are, and at that moment, you will remember who I am. Angel, this feeling is called Love, and we will feel it together. Love is powerful. You will start to glow, as I do so, Angel, that is when you will know Love. You will feel Love, just as you asked, and as I promised. Go now, my Angel.…"

She stirred in her sleep. In the background, she could hear her name being called…*Angel…Angel*…. As she stirred again, she opened her eyes and saw her brother standing over her, calling out her name and asking her to get up.

V.

ANGEL STARED UP at her brother, still groggy from sleep, with Sara by her side. As she awoke, confused thoughts were running through her mind from her dream. The dream seemed so real to her; it felt like she was actually there, wherever "there" was. She remembered being surrounded by a light that was so warm, like open arms embracing her body. Angel enjoyed being in its presence; it felt a lot like being hugged by her wonderful brother, and this gave her much joy. It was confusing, though, because she couldn't remember ever being in a place like that. But it felt so familiar to her…just as if she had been there before. With these thoughts of her dream still fresh in her mind, Angel and Adam headed off to the lake for their morning swim.

As Angel enjoyed the pleasant feel of the water around her body, she continued to think about what her dream had meant. But her dream came back to her only in clouded memories of colors, lights, and pictures. She remembered seeing rocks, and feeling many things, but wasn't quite sure what it all meant. After spending some time swimming and sitting around watching the sunrise, Adam called out to her abruptly, interrupting her thoughts, for Angel was just staring off into the distance, dreaming her dream. He was saying that he was ready to go back to the cave, and asked if she was ready to go too.

As they walked through the grassy countryside on a trail that led them to the boulder field giant boulders as big as houses, and tiny ones, too Adam spoke up. He asked Angel what was on her mind. He noticed that she had been deep in thought most of the morning, just as he had been yesterday, just as she was now.

"Angel, is there something bothering you? You look troubled. Are you worried? For now, I am worried about you."

"No, my brother. I just had a dream last night that seemed so real, but I can't seem to understand what it all meant."

Adam looked up. He saw the boulder field just ahead. He turned to his sister and said, "I'll race you to the other side. First one there gets the largest juicy strawberries!"

Angel laughed to herself, because she knew Adam would let her have the biggest strawberry anyway. As Angel finally reached the oth er side of the boulder field, Adam was standing there smiling at her. Then he asked, "Why do you always let me win?"

Angel shrugged her shoulders and said with a smile, "I don't know. I guess it makes me happy to see you smile when you win and besides, you always let me have the juiciest strawberries…every time."

They looked at each other and smiled, but did not know what to think of this wonderful joy they felt. Then Adam said, "C'mon let's go to the cave."

Angel looked up at her brother as she recalled something from her dream it was the rocks, the very rocks where they stood. She had seen them in her dream, and the joy of seeing her brother win at the mountain goat game. Adam motioned to her, interrupting her thoughts to say that he was ready to go to the valley to see the cave. Adam was very familiar with the mountains and all the trails, so he led the way to the valley where the cave was hidden. It was a long, steep, very rocky climb that made them both tired and gasping for breath, but Angel was enjoying the views they could see for miles. Most of this was new to her, because she had spent most of her time in the forest with the small animals, with all the beautiful, colorful flowers.

The trail had brought them to a very large rock that stuck up out of the ground like a giant tower. Adam and Angel were very tiny compared to this rock. Adam commented how hungry he was. Angel said she would like to stop for a rest. Adam told her that up around the tower there was a stream with lots of berry bushes that had sweet berries, like strawberries, beside it, and they could stop there to rest and eat. When they finally reached the stream, Adam said he would go to pick the berries, so Angel could rest.

While he was away, Angel found a comfortable place to sit and enjoy the coolness of the shade. She listened to the sounds the water made as it flowed by, through the rocks, twigs, and grass. This stream was the same one that flowed into the lake where they swam every morning.

When Adam finally returned with a pouch full of berries and nuts, Angel realized how hungry she was. She could hardly wait to eat those sweet, luscious berries. As Adam laid them out on the blanket, she noticed how many different kinds there were. She thought it was interesting how different the mountains were from the forest. The berries were sweet, and so very delicious sweet like sugar. It made them laugh when sweet juice ran down their cheeks, leaving red stains all over their faces. When they finished eating and laughing, they walked over to the stream to wash off and have a refreshing cool drink of water. Then they started off for the cave, somewhat full from the berry lunch they had just eaten. Adam said that they did not have much farther to go.

The trail they followed had been worn into place by all the animals that lived up here in the mountains. As they followed this trail, it wound its way higher into the valley, circling around the giant boulders and trees. The trees up here in the high valley were much different from those of the forest below. Some had white, shiny bark and little leaves that constantly moved as they glistened in the sunlight. There were other trees all around, mixed together. These trees had straight, pointy needles on their branches, instead of leaves. With their massive trunks, they looked twisted and warped, like they were hundreds of years old.

As Angel and Adam continued up the trail, the valley closed in around them, with high walls on either side. Adam turned around and said that they would have to leave the trail to hike up to the valley wall on the right. There were cliffs and crevices up there that hid the cave from below. As they started getting closer to where the cave was hidden, the climbing became a little harder. Sometimes they would have to jump from boulder to boulder, and other times they would crawl through the boulders as they lay over one another it was like crawling through tunnels. This reminded Angel of the times she had sat in the forest, watching the chipmunks and squirrels running from place to place, gathering food.

They finally made it to the ledge along the valley where the cave was. Adam decided to sit down to take a break, and Adam sat down beside him. As they looked out over the valley, they could see for miles. And when you looked way out across the valley floor, you could see the lake where they lived. But from up here, it looked more like a small pond. Angel closed her eyes to rest them from the bright sun, and as she sat there, she could feel that this was a magical place. She sensed that something wonderful was going to happen, but did not know what it was. After a few minutes of rest, Adam stood up, brushed himself off, and asked Angel if she was ready to go see the cave.

Adam led the way along the narrow ledge, holding his sister's hand. He was not sure why he was holding it they could both hike and climb like mountain goats. As they rounded some boulders blocking part of the path, the opening of the cave stood there before them. There was a feeling of mystery in the air that was welcoming. Adam turned to his sister and smiled at the delight he saw on her face at seeing it. The opening to the cave was small, large enough for only two people. Adam's heart was racing at the thought of returning to it again. He could still remember the voice he heard the last time he was here. The voice had not scared him, but the memory of it had him on edge. He turned to his sister again and said, "Shall we go inside and see what's in there?"

Angel squeezed Adam's hand, smiled, and said, "Lead the way, my dear brother." As they entered the cave together, Angel had a feeling that something wonderful was going to happen.

VI.

ADAM WAS THE first to enter the cave, pulling his sister behind. Every few feet, they would stop and let their eyes adjust to the darkness, for the cave had no light at all. They did this several times, until they were about fifty feet into the cave. They couldn't really see any farther than just a few feet or so. The cave got darker and darker as they went farther and farther into it, and if they turned around, they could see the light coming in from the mouth of the cave, making them feel a little easier about being in the dark. But after looking out into the light, they would have to wait for their eyes to readjust to the darkness so they could see again. Angel squeezed her brother's hand. She asked him if he was okay, and whether he had heard the voice again.

Adam shook his head no, and then said, "Let's look around to see if we can find anything interesting in our cave."

The cave was damp and quite cool, like a crisp mountain morning on a fall day. This air felt very good after climbing up the side of the valley wall. Adam let go of his sister's hand as he started off for the right side of the cave. As he was walking, he put out his hands to help feel his way around. When he put his hands above his head, he noticed that the cave had a lower ceiling toward the back. Adam continued to explore around the cave, feeling the roughness of the walls, and the sharp poking ceiling above. When his feet would kick something by accident or he stumbled, he would pick up the object and hold it to the light to see what it was. Every once in a while, he would find a rock that had several beautiful colors all over it. Others would sparkle in the light shining in from the mouth of the cave; some even glittered in the dark, with no light at all. These he would

keep, for he wanted to show the special one to his sister later, once they were outside in the light oh, how they would shine!

While Adam was busy exploring his side of the cave, Angel had a feeling she should turn around toward the cave opening to explore the ground right in front of her. She decided to go with this feeling, so she knelt down on her hands and knees, and she started feeling around in the dirt, huddled up on the cave floor with Sara by her side. This exploring of the cave was exciting and seemed familiar to her; it brought on a smile of past memories, but she wasn't sure why she was always so happy. As Angel felt around, she noticed how cool and silky soft the dirt was, but in other places the ground was a little rougher, all covered in smaller stones. As Angel continued to feel around in the dirt, she felt that she should look up and out, toward the cave opening. The light coming into the cave, as she knelt there in the dark, was so familiar. This vision before her brought on feelings that tugged at her heart with great joy, yet she felt sadness somehow, too. It was the kind of sadness you feel when you miss someone whom you love very much.

Angel was confused by these feelings. She did not know why her heart felt so heavy. A tear even welled up in her eye as she knelt there in the dark, looking out at the opening. The tear soon rolled out of her eye onto her face and down her cheek; the tear made it to her chin and hit the ground. When she had moved her knee to a more comfortable spot she yelled out in pain, noticing she had set her knee down on a large pointed rock. When she reached down to pick it up, it felt about the size of a small pine cone, but was as smooth as skin, as she continued to feel it. It brought a smile to her face; it felt warmer than the other rocks, and it had six sides to it. At one end there was a smooth point, and the other end was jagged and felt as though it had been broken off.

Angel wanted to see the rock a little better, but it was too dark in the cave. So she held it up in front of her to get a better view of it in the light coming in from the cave opening. As she moved it around in the light to inspect it, she could see that it was clear, like water. She continued to move it in her hands. The rock reflected little rainbows across her face. Angel thought to herself that this was no ordinary rock this was a magical rock.

When Angel yelled out from kneeling on the stone, Adam had been busy on the other side of the cave. He called out to her; he bellowed to her, asking if she was okay. When she did not answer, he started to make his way over to her to see what was wrong. When he reached her side, he knelt down and noticed that she was holding something in her hands, looking at it with deep interest. Adam could see that she had something very special it shone in the light, and it was very smooth. He watched her for a while, and then asked what she had found. She could not answer him right away because she did not really know, other than that it was a rock.

Then she said, "Let's go outside where there's more light, so we can see it better."

They stood up and half ran, half walked to get out into the light. When they reached the cave opening at the ledge of the valley wall, they faced each other with much excitement as they inspected the special stone. Adam asked if he could hold it for a minute or two, and Angel handed the rock to him. He noticed right away how warm it was, and that it was as smooth as water. Adam could tell that this was no ordinary rock; it had six sides to it, and all the sides came to a smooth point at one end. On the other end, it was jagged and very rough, like it had been broken from a larger stone. As he continued to hold it in his hands, as he looked at it, he could feel a tingly sensation moving through his hands. The sensation made him feel so alive, so full of energy, that his whole body vibrated. He then held the stone up to the light, and watched as it reflected rainbows of colors from its crystal clear center. This was truly the most beautiful stone he had ever seen, and he wanted to be part of it.

When he looked over at Angel, he could see how much she liked this stone, which he badly wanted for his own. However, Adam did not have the heart to ask if he could have it. He looked at his sister Angel, smiled, then handed the stone back to her and said, "It's beautiful, Angel. I know it will bring you joy and happiness such as you've never known."

Angel took the stone back from Adam. She looked at it once again, enjoying even more this time its smoothness and magnificent crystal clear body. As they stood there on the cliff of the valley wall, Adam looked out to see that they had only a few hours of sunlight left. He turned to his sister and said, "It is getting late we should start heading back down for home. What do you think that stone is?"

"I don't know, but when I hold it, I feel magical...so powerful, like I have more energy. My thoughts seem clearer...crystal clear. I was thinking of calling our new rock 'crystal.'"

Adam smiled back; he understood exactly what she meant. He was feeling pretty envious about the stone, and wished he had one of his own. For some people, the stone could do wonderful things that helped them to feel wiser and safer inside. But for Angel and Adam, the stone would prove to be more than just a wonderful stone. The stone had a magic to it that would help them learn something about themselves that would change their lives forever.

VII.

THE CLIMB DOWN was much easier; it did not take long to reach the spot by the stream where they had lunch earlier that day. They had used up what was left of the sunlight, so Adam decided this would be a nice place to stay the night. The grass was soft the trees would protect them from the cool mountain breezes. As Adam wandered off to look for something to eat, Angel laid out their blankets in the grass, with her buddy Sara. She was tired from the long day of hiking and decided to sit down for a rest. As she sat there resting, she pulled the crystal out of her pouch to admire it. Sara wagged her tail while Angel looked at it. She was mystified by the crystal's beauty, and the strange sensations it made in her hands. In her heart, she felt really good it was like a soft, tingly vibration. Angel heard her brother rus tling around in the bushes. As he returned, she quickly put the crystal back into her pouch, and stuffed it under her blanket.

Adam called out when he saw his sister. He said, "I hope you're hungry! I found tons of stuff for us to eat."

He sat down next to her on the blanket and they both started to eat. As Adam sat there, his thoughts took him back to the crystal. He just couldn't get out of his mind how powerful he had felt when he was holding it. A heavy thought began to disturb him, as he thought of how badly he wanted it…so badly. And even more disturbing, he felt a pressure inside to actually take the crystal from Angel he thought about stealing it. He was so ashamed of these thoughts; they bothered him and made him feel very sad. He had never felt this way before. He knew it wasn't right, but he had to have the crystal. He was afraid of how these thoughts kept running through his mind over and over and over again.

When they finished eating, they walked over to the stream. They bent over and washed their hands, and then got a drink of water they had learned a while ago that clean hands made water taste better. Angel noticed that Adam was really quiet. She could feel that he was upset inside, for his eyes didn't shine. So she simply asked, "Adam, what are you thinking about? Why are you so upset inside?"

Well, Adam couldn't tell her everything, because he felt bad about what he was thinking. He was afraid to say just how much he wanted that beautiful crystal. When he made something up to tell her, he felt even worse for lying. He just had to, though, so he let it go at that. He had lied for the very first time…his heart was a little cold in one spot, and he felt bad, so he knew that somehow he had done wrong. When they were done at the stream, they returned to the camping spot. The three of them curled up in the blankets, Adam and Angel and Sara all together.

Angel fell right to sleep; she was really tired from their long hike to the cave. But Adam just lay tossing and turning, he was so upset. The crystal was on his mind; thoughts of taking it troubled him deeply. But he just couldn't get out of his mind how beautiful the crystal was it was so wonderful, how it made him feel when he held it in his hands. Adam noticed the sky was starting to lighten, and then he realized he hadn't slept a wink all night. He decided to get up. He needed to relieve himself, for he drank a lot of water before bed. Then he would get something to eat for Angel and Sara, but only after he washed his hands. He did not really feel like eating much for breakfast, but he thought Angel would want to eat before heading home.

When he returned with the berries and nuts, he noticed that Angel was not in her blanket. He just figured she must be out in the trees, as he had needed to do earlier. Sara was gone, too. The dog was always by her side, so maybe she had decided to have a look around and explore the mountain forest, as she and Sara always did. Angel was always looking out for small animals in the forest; she was probably curious about what kind of creatures lived in the location where they had camped.

Adam sat down on the blankets and started picking at the berries and nuts; he didn't feel like eating because the crystal was still on his mind. As he sat there thinking, he decided to have a look at it while Angel was gone. He felt around the blankets until he found Angel's pouch. He could feel it was in there, so he pulled out the crystal. Adam's eyes widened with delight as he looked at it. He could feel his hands start to tingle from its magical energy, which was even stronger than before. He put the pouch back under the blanket, and then he sat back down on his own blanket with the crystal still in his hands. He spent several moments there absorbing the energy from the crystal, watching it glisten in the morning sun. Oh, how he enjoyed the reflections and rainbow colors it made in the morning light!

As he was sitting there, he heard a noise in the background that startled him. He figured it would be Angel returning, but he did not want her to see him with the crystal that he had taken out of her pouch. As the noises got closer, he figured he would not have time to put the crystal back, so he slipped it under his blanket as quickly as he could. Doing that made his heart race as if he had climbed a mountain.

Just then, Angel (with Sara, as always) stepped into the camp where Adam was witting. She looked at her brother and said, "You should see some of the animals out there in the forest they're so cute. Sara loves to chase them all around. I was sitting by the trail eating when a furry little creature stopped by to watch me and Sara. I took one of the nuts I had and held it out for the animal to see it was so cute; the little guy took the nuts from my hand and just sat there eating with me, but as soon as the nut was gone, poor Sara was bursting to run. I had to hold her back. I think she wanted to have some more fun again, and she chased the animal all over the forest."

She continued to explain that the animals were a little different up here than they were down by the lake in the forest, but they were just as friendly and cute. Angel was in a joyful mood; it made her feel good to be with the animals. Adam asked her if she was ready to head home. Angel nodded, and so they started packing their things. Adam was relieved that she hadn't given any thought to the crystal, and just packed the pouch along with everything else. It really bothered him that he had taken it, but he couldn't face the idea of returning the crystal he would feel so embarrassed about what he had done.

It took most of the afternoon to hike the rest of the way down the mountain, and back home. They were both hot and pretty sweaty at this point, so they decided to take a swim. In their excitement to reach the lake and cool off, they threw their things down and made a mad dash for the lake. They spent several hours splashing and play ing in the water, as if they'd never done it before. It was a beautiful evening in the land of heaven's valley; the water felt refreshing, and the air was warm.

As they climbed out of the lake, Angel said, "Let's run! I will race you back to the spot where we left our things."

Of course, Adam was a fast runner, but he let her win so she could dry off first. While they were drying off, Sara was also drying off by shaking her fur. She was getting Adam and Angel wet again. They tried to chase her off, but Sara thought they wanted to play. They stood there, and oh, how they laughed as Sara danced around and spun; she shook her tail around, yelping and barking as she dried her fur.

The sun was setting low on the horizon behind the clouds as it painted the sky with all the beautiful colors of earth. Angel real ly enjoyed watching the sunsets somehow they seemed magical. Her heart, she knew, would feel the music inside herself as the sun dropped in musical tones just beyond and behind the mountains in the distance. She loved how the sun would sing. As they both sat down to watch the setting sun, Angel commented on how beautiful it was tonights.

Adam agreed as he asked, "How do you suppose all of this came about the forest, these beautiful mountains, the animals, each day, the wonderful sunsets? I'd never really thought about it before, but it is a mystery, wouldn't you say?'

Angel replied, "I'm not really sure, Adam, but I remember having dreams of a place that was much like this. It was just as warm as this place, just as colorful…it had a beauty that I can't even describe; it felt like I had been there before. It also felt as though there were a presence around me, and I was being hugged. It made me feel warm, and really safe."

Angel stopped talking. She noticed that her skin was bumpy and kind of tingly; it wasn't a cold feeling, but a warm feeling that went through her whole body. Her throat felt tight, and she couldn't talk any more about the dream. These memories brought out feelings that were so real, so powerful she had to stop.

When Adam heard her stop talking, she sounded different, and he looked to see what was wrong. As he looked at her face, he noticed a wet streak running down her cheek. He thought maybe she was hurt, and he asked if she was okay. Angel smiled and nodded yes, then continued to watch the setting sun. Adam decided to move closer to her, to help comfort her and make her feel better.

As the sun was about to drop down behind the mountains, Angel had the idea to get out her crystal. She was thinking about how beauti ful it would be to see the sunset through the crystal's clear body. She moved over to where her blanket was, and started searching around for her pouch. When she found the pouch, a rush of panic went through her body like a hot flash the crystal was gone. She continued to search through her things for the crystal, but it wasn't anywhere to be found. She knelt there wondering what could have happened to it.

As she was searching, Adam was off to the side, watching her. He was now feeling bad that he had taken her crystal. But for some reason, he just couldn't admit to her that he had taken it. He thought to himself that he hadn't really intended to take it Angel just surprised him when she returned from the forest; he had not wanted her to see him admiring the crystal, so he quickly stuffed it under his blanket. He had planned to return it to the pouch when she wasn't looking, but he never had the chance to put it back. He felt so bad now; he could not bring himself to say anything. Oh, how he wished it would all go away! He had no way to turn back time.

Angel moved back to where her brother was sitting, to finish watching the sunset. As she sat there watching, she wondered what could have happened to the crystal. She was sure that she had put it back in the pouch before going to sleep last night. Then she thought it might have fallen out somewhere along the trail, or maybe somewhere at the campsite when she'd thrown her things down to go for a swim. It was too dark now to try to find it, so she would just have to wait until morning.

The sun was completely down behind the mountains now, so Angel decided she would go to bed. She turned to Adam and said, "Adam, I'm going to bed. In the morning, will you help me find my crystal? It is not in its pouch, and I can't find it anywhere with my things."

As she always did, Sara curled up with Angel to keep warm. Adam nodded his head and said he would be happy to help her search, but deep down inside he was feeling really terrible about what he had done. Adam soon followed his sister to bed, but it was useless he couldn't get to sleep, feeling the way he did. After lying there for a long time listening to Angel sleeping, he came up with an idea that would fix everything.

VIII.

THE NEXT MORNING when Angel stirred from her sleep, she noticed that Adam had already gotten up and was gone. Angel lay there for a while, petting Sara. She liked her ears rubbed, as dogs do. Angel lay on her blanket wondering what could have happened to the crystal. She was also trying to recall something from her dream, but it was clouded with other thoughts and memories. What she could remember of the dream was a picture of someone hugging another person. She felt happy in the dream, but the other person was sad and crying. She figured it must have been her, hugging someone who was heart broken, but she didn't know why.

Angel felt something under her blanket that brought her out of her thoughts. When she rolled over, she reached under the blanket and found something very familiar it was the crystal! She smiled briefly because she had found it, but was puzzled about how it had gotten there. She was sure that it hadn't been there last night. She scratched her head and gave Sara a puzzled look, wondering if she might know something.

Angel stood up and called out to Sara. "Come on, Sara let's go find Adam. Let's tell him the good news about finding the crystal."

Angel and Sara went out searching along the trail for Adam, thinking he must be out looking for the crystal himself, for he knew how much Angel loved this wonderful rock. As they went along, Angel would pick up sticks and throw them for Sara to fetch. Sara would faithfully return every time with the same stick to be thrown again. Sara was such a delight to watch Angel would sometimes laugh over her friend's silliness. When Sara returned once more with the stick, Angel took it from her and threw it out way over the top of a large boulder. Sara ran after the stick. When she rounded the boulder, she saw Adam sitting there on a rock. Sara jumped around, wagging her tail she was happy and licking Adam all over because she was excited to see him. Then she ran back to Angel, barking to let her know that she had found Adam, just in case Angel could understand her.

When Angel rounded the boulder, she saw Adam sitting with his back to the trail. Angel called out, "Adam, we've been looking for you I found the crystal!" Angel couldn't help noticing that Adam seemed upset about something; his shoulders were shaking as if he were laughing, but it wasn't laughter she heard…he was trembling with pain, because he knew he had lied.

Through sobs of sadness, Adam replied, "I know."

Angel sat down beside him to see if he was okay; she wanted to make sure he wasn't hurt. As she sat there looking him over, she asked, "How would you know I found the crystal? You were gone when I woke up."

Adam wiped the tears from his face and then said, "I knew you would find the crystal because I put it there under the blanket."

"Well, when did you find it? You could have waited until I got up to give it to me."

"Angel, you don't understand. I didn't find it I took it from you. I really liked the crystal a lot, and it was making me want it all the time. It made me feel good…stronger, even powerful. While you and Sara were gone the other morning, I took the crystal out of your pouch to look at it. When I heard you returning I didn't want you to see me admiring it, so I just slipped it under my blanket. I meant to give it back, but you were always carrying your pouch, so I couldn't put it back. And then last night when you were looking for the crystal, I thought that maybe you would think you had lost it on the trail. I really wanted to keep it, but it hurt too much inside when I saw how sad you were about losing it."

Adam broke out into another fit of sobbing and weeping, and tried to blurt out that he was sorry. Angel didn't know what to think. She was confused. She felt happy for finding the crystal, but was sad because her brother felt so badly about what he had done. With the confusion running around in her mind, she started to recall parts of her dream. In the dream she felt happy too, but also remembered hugging someone who was really sad. She finally realized that the sad person in her dream must have been Adam. He was heartbroken and she was trying to console him, in the dream. At this thought, and seeing her brother before her now, her heart clenched with new feelings she had never felt before. As she put her arm around Adam to comfort him, a new word popped into her mind, and it said: *Remember.* There was a pleasant feeling that went along with the word and went through her body, making her take note.

As she closed her eyes to push out the tears from this feeling and tried to make some sense of the dream, she realized that these were not dreams at all…they were memories. These were memories of a time long ago. She recalled seeing colors brighter than sunsets, a light that was warm and so very comforting, a sense of being lighter and more free while moving around. There were memories of conversa tions running through her mind, which went on endlessly.

As she sat there thinking about this and comforting Adam, the same word kept flashing in her mind. *REMEMBER, Angel… REMEMBER.*

Angel was trying to remember what she needed to remember, but her whole body was being tormented with feelings, and many new sensations that she had never felt before. These feelings were power ful, pushing and clenching at her heart, sending tingly vibrating warm pulses throughout her body, making her feel like she was part of the

WHOLE universe and everything around her. She didn't understand these feelings, but they felt so wonderful…she hoped they would never end. She wished she could take away Adan's hurt and all his pain she wanted to share with him what she was feeling. Then she remembered that all his pain started because of the crystal.

Angel put out her other arm. She wrapped it around him to show that she wasn't upset with him at all. She could feel his hurt and all his disappointment, so she held on to him tighter to try to take it away. When she was able to clear her throat and speak she said, "Dear brother, everything is okay, for I LOVE YOU." Angel's eyes popped open at the sound of what she had said. She had remembered!

Adam wiped back his tears, smiled, and said, "I love you too, Angel. I don't know why I did it, but I am very sorry."

Angel took the crystal from her pouch. She handed it to Adam and said, "I know why, Adam, and someday you will, too. You will know what I know. Thank you for helping me to remember."

God smiled down on them as Adam and Angel were embracing one another for comfort. Angel noticed a flash of light out of the corner of her eye. Although it was daylight, it reminded her of a twinkling star. This bright flash put a smile on her face that made her laugh. Adam looked up at the sound of her laughter and with watery eyes and a big smile, Adam said, "You're welcome."

As Sara sat by impatiently waiting for Angel and Adam, the forest around them filled with animals and creatures of all kinds. There were hundreds of them. Sara could see birds in the trees, chipmunks and squirrels in the grass, rabbits on the rocks, and even deer farther back in the forest. It appeared as if all of God's creatures could sense the energy of their love and were here to see what was about to happen.

As the animals watched, they could see the forest start to glow brighter, and then the sunlight around them. The light was coming from the center of the circle where they had gathered. Angel and Adam were still embracing in Angel's forgiving, unconditional Love. As they continued to watch, the light grew brighter and brighter. Sara let out a bark that got the attention of all the other animals. When they turned their eyes back to the center, the light shot up into the sky with a streak. It looked like a shooting star falling to earth, or a comet shooting across the skies. Quick as a flash, Angel and Adam were no longer in the center of their circle.

Angel looked at God and smiled. She had never seen God glow as brightly as he did now. The two of them embraced in the harmony of their pure Love, and Angel said, "Thank you for sharing your Love with me, Father now I know what Love feels like, and who we truly are. Can we do it again?" she asked with a smile.

With God's wink and a flash, Adam knew what she meant, that someday he too would know what he felt God's Love, and that Love is what everyone will be. Adam was then pulled into the light to embrace his sister. In an instant, he too was intertwined in God's light of love.

BOOM! CRASH! SMASH! With a flash, God burst into the universal rainbows of light of Love and pure joy, for his children understood his Love, the pure Love planet was made, and God now knew his plan was working. As God floated into the heavens, he whispered back to Angel and Adam, "Now listen up, my children my plan is now complete for you all to Be of Love. Angel, now listen your new name is Eve, for you are the mother of all to be. Adam, you will always be the man you are, for your free will and choice are yours to be. Eve is pure she was made from Angel, who is ME…she lives in love and she will never stray. So, Adam, try to follow Eve, for she is the light of Love and she is Me. The heart you have is beating in tune with me and my Love, and if you should sway in your play from the

men of wrong and plenty, then try to listen to the Love of Eve. Pay close attention and listen to what she says. When and if you should fall astray into the wrongs of men who want to sway you from my Love, then remember that if you feel lost, I have a safety plan for you."

Eve said, "When I pray, God will send messengers and prophets to us. They will help us to remember that peace and love are our way. Now listen up, my new man to be…we will have God's children together in our play. God said that a princess with dark brown skin will be our first, and she will be as pure as I am. When she is 25,000 years old, after we teach our Love in many ways, then she will fly away. With God's seed she will go to Africa, and she, as we did, will teach Love just as we learned it from our Father God. She will show her offspring to be all the same Love from above the Love and joy with peace in all things, for this is God's joy. Now Adam, this is our quest for God; you see as well in all the families to be we will learn and teach this Love for God, for he said he will return for all those that learn how to play with Love."

Now remember, when you go out to play all you need to know is that Love is the only way to play! The peace planet Earth emerges; the universe is saved!

Your Bible My Bible Their Bible

Hello. I love you all, and I Am. In the beginning, where would one even begin to share or start a story like this? Where would one start, considering there is nothing to begin with…just a blank, empty slate of nothingness…maybe it isn't black at all, maybe just clear lights of eternal harmony, but for now, a nothing that simply emerges from a clean, black empty slate. If the Divine creator of creation built solely for eternal life based on Love, could or would that God say anything at all? And if so, would any of you pay attention to his/her notes left in a book for us to find, or just believe in thanks to the everyday miracles of life on display? Would the creator even come to terms with words easily read, for you to learn my explanation of life's origins? I won der, for if my beings are awake and conscious, then the words of our worlds written in books would not be needed at all. Apparently the evidence of our lives is not enough proof for any of us that we are God's, and made by God.

Then, in light of the Divine creation, would God say, "Why do I need to write the story of myself, of us, and you? For isn't your life enough evidence that you are of the Divine life force source, for there you are?" So, where is a reasonable place to begin with writ ten words, for a story like this that anyone could easily grasp in the complete understanding of your individual God created life? All of you are extensions of a vision…or possibly your/our God could have started here with these few words of cosmic origins. What could then be written when life's miracles are unseen? There are no impossibili ties that can exist at all, for it is God's probabilities in his/her infinite imaginative creation of his/her/our inevitable eternal Life.

In this text, God is possibly revealing the origins of the very God particle of creation…is possibly speaking now, in this moment, in our shared time. This is in fact a never ending story of possibilities yours, mine, ours or God's message of how we came to be. So in any imagination, we would then understand the God particle's writ ten word of creation. It would be understood in and by us all. Would you then believe or bother to hear his/her voice, or even feel what is written? Is God speaking to us, to you? So then certainly, maybe and evidently, because all possibilities do exist, so this entity, our God, did come to biological form and then did write down this true mo ment of words. The absolute split second of creative consciousness of life is when this tiny invisible speck, the God particle this tiny dot awakened and came to be all of you. Would you believe what's written is of you, all from the One?

Without a doubt, you understand completely in your spirit that this is the very first pinpoint of conscious creation of God. Kindly, with respect of us and words well, let's just say for instance it is you and God, our God, the very first God of all there is and will always be, for this God dot is infinite within itself and in its own creations, in and our our/your/its individual creation of all things, your life. How this God dot, this is your/our/his/her eternal life source of pure Divine eternal life creation. Well, in the first moment, it must be simply sit ting in the pure, empty dark matter, absolutely awakened and con scious of the now moment in our creation. God is now manifesting you from itself, all of it all, every entire speck of you and me or better yet, simply floating around in its singular yet infinite individu alities of superconsciousness as its awareness is in great depth every creative notion of pondering about us all is simply creating it all.

Our God dot particle is sitting so far, far away in formulation of it all. His consciousness, this puny dot of us all that exists in you, is of me, this infinite dot...it is in everything you see, everything you imag ine. This God dot is the creation of me through you, and all we create in God. We as one in the individual forms of you are of us all; we as God will recreate in our never ending perepetual life cycle unto eternity. I, he/she of us all within this creator reaches farther than the bands of deepest darkness that your physical evidence shows to you. I am that which is surrounding all life well, that is, once life really happens that is for us all, you all, and it all.

For now, the God dot of all is just an open conscious thought just a black, crystal clean dark slate matter of space...nothing at all, just purity in thought of it all. The only thing that there could ever be first is just this tiny, tiny microbe of a molecule, which simply has recognized its consciousness of itself, for I am this little spot of a dot, yet even I am 400,000,000,000 times smaller than this simple dot you see (.) this puny microbe of a dot, and I am infinite in my size. You have all grown to ignore this; I see within all of you who with pure carelessness brazenly disbelieve our God this is part of the Divine design. This is of me, and life's origin is simply you all, but for you this dot (.) so far is nothing at all, because nothing has yet to be defined or created in any way, shape, or form nothing exists at all except for me.

Evidently to us all or just to me, and possibly US all long be fore this particular point in time (and yes, even our God's first thought of consciousness), as a matter of fact there is another particular dot particle of unified singular consciousness that has come to realize in its simple recognized point of conscious time that I am this first dot of dots to be. For I am aware that there is another significant pinpoint of time where it simply all began. This particular moment of time is long before its consciousness of our God's time, or of when our time was even aware of its own infinite possibilities, long before you and I even appear on paper or came to be a simulated thought of any kind. This pinpoint in our birth moment of time is well beyond your dreams, simply hidden deep in your unconscious or by now, your some what hidden consciousness of unknown awareness of your Divine creation, and our God's creation, for that thought of I Am from within is his first thought of recognition of his own split off life created in consciousness from the pure light by which his creation as well as ours will be protected.

We must all sit in complete wonder, and ponder with all our imaginations what it all is. Without fear, we must simply imagine all we can be from what we see. All our faith began in the same place, and yet we have ended up in such a mixed up, hateful division of their original pure created purpose. We are all living in disbelief of the inner pure life God source. We are making our lives very hard, without love or peace shared in any of our faiths created by God here on earth. We are blinded by not seeing God within, as we blankly stare back into that time when We or It may have been the very origin of God's biological creation, but that truth is hidden by our inner unbelief.

As we you and I, and almost anyone, I believe can see, we are of the Divine life source, for we see that everything created comes from the I AM. As we pour out our denial of what should unite us in faith, our thoughts are now not pure, but are poured into the light of God; we pour our thoughts into our songs, which we sing in the lan guages of individual belief, not in the united harmony that God pre fers, as God planned. So as we are all peering through the darkness, we can only imagine where it all began for you and me. This is your book to show that I am you, for we are all of God, and you are me.

God's consciousness is awakened in us.

This dot molecule recently mentioned may be God, sitting in the heavy darkness, for now he/she is silent…very silent and quiet. In a flash of infinite consciousness, in an instance of light, God is suddenly aware. He/she is awakened with a flash of superior evolved supercon sciousness of a multitude of never ending creations of multiverses, which in a collective universe the God of all has created our God of you all. Thus in perpetual creation, God is now perfectly quantified in his/her consciousness of I Am. Our life source is awakened now in our God. God has split unto God; God is Godding Gods unto you. This tiny God dot suddenly awakens into the creation of everything yet again in eternal creation, so then our God suddenly emerges in an instant, at our now never ending pinpoint of time, and unto you are the Gods.

Hey! Hey, look at me! I am aware of all my darkness I am aware that it is all Me. I am so beautifully thick and slick with an infinite number of free flowing possibilities in all imagined potential of man kind; I am so very smooth. I am smooth as glass, pure and perfect as black onyx, so perfectly pitch black silky smooth, not a flaw to be seen or felt, not a tear, crack, or ripple in my ever so flawless darkness of me. Look at all I am so very clean and sleek; you simply can't compare the darkness to blackness of any kind, for we know not yet what it all is or what it will ever be. There are no scars on me yet to show up on my silky clean black ME, the eternal darkness of I Am. You see, my heavy dark mass is of I Am this I Am that is seem ingly flowing throughout the cosmos here and there…it's everywhere; I am everywhere and everything. There is no lighter shade of gray, or blacker black, just me. Pure pitch glossy black is my space covering everything; what you see is you and me. Like the rivers and oceans of our planet that effortlessly flow with my earthly magic, my rivers and oceans simply cover Earth as it sits spinning and floating in this silky black darkness that is certainly covering up most all of everything you see, from beyond our visible visions within the darkness that con sumes the cosmos, and beyond this darkness it smothers and covers the universe. This, we can see, is all of me. I Am.

My darkness you see is the darkness that protects all things. Only the light of good can pass through the darkness and into the realm of good or the peaceful light of God's true home for you all to be to exist and live eternally. My new black slate is simply clean and pure no light, no color, no biological forms…just a perfect, clean black slate. So much to fill, so much to be, so much to paint of all the individu als to be me…so many unique forms of I to test. Nobody enters my Divine heaven without passing through the dark mass of I Am. There is nothing to see or feel or touch or taste…oh, what will it all be? What could it all be? When will it all be? Why me? You will all see; life will soon be.

I am God, the God of your lives and all lives ever to be are of me; this you will see. No other life can be, without me in it. Your lives are all a matter of me in biological form, as well as of me in synthetic form or otherwise. It is all me in there I am you, and all of you will be this…you will all see. Suddenly there will be instant awareness a light of tremendous energy is born. Boom! This is what has been done; I've split off into two halves. This is what I can do, just like you can do as well. I am the dot of Love; I am all Eternal Life. Through this Love and peace you will all see what is to be, and you will succeed. Your life is a complete transfer of the pure, open free life force of me. I have come to split into two halves, you see, for my one first son to be just as you are, in time.

He is my pure son, the first of two, Lucifer of the Divine darkness, the one and only gatekeeper of the Divine access to my lighted and pure domain. For then as I Am of the Divine light of pure, uncondi tional loving creation of both realms. I am the spark of life that in awareness of it all starts right here, for there is nothing beyond this point, or in other words, there is nothing beyond our point of time. This is your beginning; this is the first point in any time of all time. This is to be until your personal evolution of love in complete learned creations of soul and character, and you can then return to the pyra mid of God's infinite planted seed particle atop the pyramid, to the very points of creation then and only then, with pure Love on all levels of Love, you can enter the Divine, and then you will be as I am, and can recreate yourself. You must evolve in pure, lighted Love in order to quantify our life systems of creation, when you all return to this pinpoint of time in purity, you will have all come home to my home in the purity of choice, purity of spirit, then to your home, your true home. Your home will now be ready for you to be Gods; your self transformation will be complete, evolution in motion. The light of creation is your home, and we are one when you return.

I will always be waiting for you in this light of Love this is for you, all that I have made. You will all see that you can do just as I have created all of you, you will all be and see that when you all return into the light of creation, then together, as one in the pure eternal form, we activate the multiverse of God particles, and we then all split in unison into the next dimensions of our new cre ations of enlightened human Gods. My son Lucifer of the Divine darkness is floating above all my inventions in heaven's skies; he is the protector of the Divine light. You must break free of the dark and come to eventually master the pure light of creation. Lucifer is my other half; our created dark son Lucifer of the heavenly precious dark is the design of the Divine to protect it all to protect the life source energy. Now, again, in a God instant I split him into two, and out of one half I formed a pure brother of pure white light. The one pure light Son of Love was born, and they were brothers in my plan and you will see how they will protect the Divine. I am both of them now you see, I am all of them, I am everything that is to be, and I am within you all, as you will see. I am both the spark of light and the lack of light in darkness; I am the light of you all, so you call me God.

In my vision of our lives, my pure second son will be your peaceful guide. My son of the purest lighted love is Jesus. This son is of pure light, pure form, unconditional Love…pure freedom and eternal life of peace within. This son will be at the doorway of my pure domain of all my doorways and domains unto eternal life in universal pure Love, through Lucifer, and then Jesus, for if the door opens from the dark unto the light of Jesus, then I will be certain of your proven purity free upon entry to the Divine, for you will have mastered your conscious ness…you have mastered the deceptions of Lucifer and given unto the unconditional love of Jesus, for then I know that my son Lucifer has sent you into the realm of Jesus' pure light of Love, and in purity you are now awakened by my two sons, and you are now like me in pure God form congratulations!

My invention of Lucifer, who is pure darkness, I have commanded in his life choices to temper you until all hell has been burnt out of you. You know by now that my Lucifer is solely invented to protect all of you the very light is protected by all of Lucifer's evil dark tempta tions of many offered to the unevolved pure lights of you. Eventually you will see this, and your consciousness will realize the very reasons why I chose this way. For you see, I am all three, as I am all the indi vidual particles inside the three, as I am all of your particles as well.

Surely you will come to know this, in pure consciousness. You will see that I am in it all…this I am. I am at once the God of Lucifer and the God of Love. I am the Dot (.) of Everything. I am that is within it all, and within you all, all things great and small. I am the very one of all that's all of US all.

This new God Dot is a God evolved from a multiverse of gods, from a pure Divine quantum split of the very Divine God to be. So this new dot or God split from a new I or he, and them himself again split into two out of one pure as I of you. Now you see this perpetual creation in motion of all, for he knew for certain and you will also see in your pure God form to be that there is one thing for sure: in his very own consciousness of his own created awakening in this moment, his moment, all our moments of being, all moments of continuation of being in any form, especially in God form, for he now knew where it all began…therefore this original design of our Divine particle must be protected at any costs. For he as in you and I have returned in our own pure biological dynamics of different quantified life forms of awareness consciousness of faiths, of colors in and of our true parallel universes of original creation from the one.

So, as his new universe and our new universes split into his or our new multiverse, then into a quantum split, this is a perpetual creation in motion of us as gods, just like he knew he himself was born or created from the most Divine light of creation. So on his arrival, he knew for sure that for himself to be and for all to be as his own inven tion of his creation, there must be a design of perfect protection an absolute perfect design to protect it all, simply for the continuation of our perpetual creation, in teaching all there is to teach for all of you to become gods, as he and you are one, and have become us all. Our God knew he had foreseen that he must first be protected, himself, from all bad things, only to ensure that he himself has protected the original creator of his creations and ours, who are of his very own in vention, as well as within all creations in order to split from the God dot as the never ending eternal life of biological creations for then this that we all are could never end, for as you see, we are still in it. This must be protected at any cost.

This eternal triangle paradigm of Gods is your soul's purifica tion its transformation from evil into the pure light of love, into God's creation of biological forms to exist as Gods in the physical realms of touch, sound, feelings, emotions, and love in the eternal, perpetual, biological God in the flesh of your body's forever eternal life mastered for then, you are now eternal.

In order to create a foolproof system, the darkness was created as a rite of passage to test all characters to test all who attempt their individual clear path entry into God's domain, for you are created in the pure light form of love first. God's consciousness is awakened in all lighten beings; within all biological creations of my domain, they will be created in my form first, in my many biological human forms. To exist together individually as one, I see our life through you in all my multitude of universes. There will be many extensions of life in many ways, many solar systems, and within them all there will be many species who are like you, and who will attain the same eternal life path for all. This, as you will come to see, is happening on many planets, where there are many lives with many suns similar to where I'm from we are all each other, and I live within it all.

Illustration: Lucifer vs. Jesus, dividing the pure from the impure souls

ANGEL AND ADAM

Now listen, and try to imagine how this system of darkness vs. pure light works. I've created this path of purity through the temptations of the dark, for free choice is yours yes, of course the dark is run by Lucifer himself, for he has been created for a complete and complex test designed with a multitude of checkpoints and balances so that you can evolve into a pure state, for you must be pure in resolution within your spirit, and filled with pure trust, peace, and love. You must be infinite in divine purification before entry. From the spirit of free choice, you have now become one with the one who leaves the prison of darkness formed from free will and choices, who has ascended by open consciousness and can enter the lighted domain of creation this pure spirit can only pass into the light if the darkest tests of purification of darkness exhumed from within you have awakened with the very creation that resulted in your purity. If a soul or spirit contains even a speck of evil made by Lucifer, that soul or spirit cannot come into the presence of God's pure light of all creation.

Your purity is a process of choice dark vs. light so you must be pure of choice, pure of love, for then and only then can you rise to the top of God's Divine pyramid of life. The triangles of creation will never contain impure spirits or dark souls. You have an eternity of reincarnations to cycle from birth into the choice of purity or darkness. Eventually you will come to purity, for I, God, am at the top of the triangle. In your process of choosing light over dark, or good over evil, you will all ebb and flow into these choices until you all reach purity at the top, for we remain connected all of us are attached to my auras of lighted energy, just as our original Creator sits in slumber as well, connected by strands of light that attach our love light creation. This God waits, as I myself sit and wait for you all, until you awaken into purity from free choice.

Then the Gods will stir I will stir in open consciousness with you all in your awakening within your individual faiths of con sciousness, as one pure love completion, our God then as I am your God. I have done this in pure creation as you will all be, so will I be of God. He and I and we in purity will all burst as the order of one into two then three, into fourfold multipyramids, spiraling in explosive perpetual life. This is our plan in our pure creation from love and harmony this you will be; you all will be as I am, and the Divine…we are never ending creations of purity. This, you see, is all we can be, with me at the top of God's gate of creation, you are of your very own triangles of creation in a quantified reality of universes to be this version of you will achieve being gods, just as I have become God to you.

Now listen, all you who have lost your way. This was written for you to find one day. I've left this book out here just for you to find, hidden inside the very trunk of this old oak tree this is the Tree of Life and Truth. This book of words shall never be lifted from the light ed circle around the tree of your life and the truth of me, for the pages of words within, you will not be able to read if you open it outside the lighted circle that surrounds this Tree of Life.

You have all been created from the heavens above, from my dis play. All you see is all I am this is simply you. All within and without me, we are one and the same. You are all in the body of my image; you are the very DNA or stardust of the heavens; you are the pure lights of my unconditional Love. You and all the creations of our universe I am connected to it all and so are all of you. Like the blood in your veins, I flow within it all, and you flow within it all. Love is the ultimate connection to it all. Everything you see and do not see, in biological entity form, as well as the synthetic invisible life forms are all of you, and me.

You have been created with free flowing forms of faith and choice, pure loving unconditional consciousness of me is within you. The pyramid of life depends solely on unification in purifica tion of the Divine spirits and souls here on earth. You must be at peace, activated by Love for me and for all of you, to achieve peace within all of the differences we share in all forms of creation you within the one are to unconditionally love all of you. This book is for all the biological forms of Earth, or those who pass through Earth's universal peace portal unto eternal life, for we are the key to it all, just as in my creator's multiverse there is another planet, a twin of Earth, just like our Planet Earth. The biological forms of my father have successfully mastered the peace star planet's injection of Love into his own multiverse; this God achieved activation of universal peace in his domain, thus in activation unto our domain, for then God is born now atop our life pyramid, so within that pyramid of God's creations, unto our God they now wait in suspended, ampli fied tones of Love, pure lighted consciousness, they wait for us to purify our pyramid of creation.

You see now that our planet, our Earth, has been chosen as the Pure Star Planet of Peace. It has been chosen by design, simple cre ated for our universal peace process, but its activation is up to us.

Earthlings are the singular key to universal purification of all lives in this triangle of perpetual creation of you and me. All biological creations of our universe, by design, will have to travel here too, and though Earth is the only point of access to the Divine Creator's do main, our job on Earth is to realize that we must come together in peace to succeed in the unification of spirits and souls. Bearing our creation of pure truth in this, then it is to have Lucifer, my son, who has given his soul to be the one energy anointed with the pure bless ings of control over all biological universal forms, as well as all plan ets, solar systems, and universal controls, in order to separate the pure from the impure.

You see, the only way to recreate a new creation of us into the multiverse, and then quantify ourselves into a splitting of new life paradigms and perpetual creations, is only by the pure evolution of biological forms into complete love in purity. Lucifer, who is as I am, is incomplete for remember, I split half of life unto him and unto you in order to be. This half of me also exists in all molecules, in all DNA in all these chemicals inside you, we are one and the same. This is why we are one and the same, for each life has choices and chances of pure light or pure dark, to be what you choose to be. If a biological form is to be more of me and mostly me, choosing in all good, in all light, in perfect unconditional Love with pure form visible tones and lights of pure open consciousness well, if this form or dot (yes, a God dot) as you all are comes to be, and if it were to be God in pure form, then this energy would be transferred into the purification of our life's universal triangles of God, as shown in the diagram following. It is Lucifer's job to give you great tests for your soul, character, and spirit. He will tempt and test you in many ways, with his false books of faith yes, books written about me to fool you, and these fabled and miswritten ways will try to deceive your path of creation.

Why, you ask? This is an absolute must, in order to see your heart clearly. Only then can you enter the Divine, for if Lucifer can lead you astray, then you are still incomplete, and you will be sent back for another rebirth where you can exercise free will, with a chance of eternal life. Do not worry; the purification of souls was created and needed to ensure the moment when the universe will cascade into the pyramids of our then perpetual four ply multi quantified verse. Then multiply it by eight it can happen only in the purity of the pure souls and spirits created by free choice and free will. If the entire mass of souls with an awakened pure light spirit of love awaken, only then can the split occur then, as we push into the four ply universe, spun into an eight ply universe. In its purification, it is then quantified to split off into creations of multiple universes… eight to sixteen to thirty two, etc., and per petual life continues.

So, if we fail and Lucifer succeeds in the perpetual reincarnation of returned impure souls, we and I and the pure will be in perpetu al motion as well. We will be sending prophets and messengers of many colors and designs. These prophets will be there to fight against Lucifer's persistent pleasures in keeping you lost from your eventual life's destiny, which is the mission to purify your spirit entry into our universes with a complete transformation of biological entities into free form gods.

The Peace/Love paradigm begins on the peace star Planet Earth, the very center of our triangulated life source. This is the only way for you as a God biological form to achieve eternal life, through the purification of souls. You, they, all of us must pass through the planet, which birthed biological forms into gods. Your purification is under no time constraint; this is an individual evolution of self in purity, of recognized self in me and others. It is our purification. You see, at the end of this never ending life, you have free will to live in the dark and be just that, or you can choose transformation of purity into the Divine light. When that happens, you are enlightened, then all can come unto you, and you can be with me in eternal life. If there is still Lucifer or darkness in you, then you cannot pass into the eternal light. You are US; we are the center of the universal pyramid of our universe's creation of us. Eventually you will all evolve into individual universes of your own Divine creations, as I am in you. You have free will to choose whether to evolve in the pure light of creation, or remain in perpetual decay. Many entities from every where must pass through our peace planet Earth to enhance our God made creations. All life forms on Earth must first be cleansed before the created souls can join the triangle of gods rising up in our purification free form processes. The only hidden secret for all this to be is…

All forms will give unconditional Love. When Love honors the Love of all forms, evil will change to peace. We sweep the planet with all the Love I've shown, which I teach for your entry into my domain. Only through the purification of souls can you evolve into pure God form. Purify your universe…not just your soul, but the souls of everyone.

Judge not, but honor all

Cheers to our future in eternal life through peace, with unconditional, infinite awareness that all faiths end up on God's doorstep. Live individually as you are, but in a united individualism to our bio logical eternal evolution.

I do so love you all. I, David G. Bicker, have devoted my soul to our planet of biological universal peace. I am God as you are God; he made us all from himself, a pure life source. Peace and Love are eternal life anything less is LESS!

God bless us all each soul that is, or will be.

My deepest vision is of a man who invents the Earth paradigm's first free city. By design, I have a plan that requires you only to be civil and peaceful, and you can be anointed into Earth's first freedom city…coming soon.

Thank you.

May God bless all there is.

www.ingramcontent.com/pod-product-compliance
Lightning Source LLC
LaVergne TN
LVHW020431080526
838202LV00055B/5121